On the Day You Were Born

Sophie Piper ✫ Kristina Stephenson

LION
CHILDREN'S

On the day you were born
you were very small,
very special

and very clever.

From day one you could do lots of things.

breathing and sleeping

waking and
looking

You taught us all to understand your little noises. Whatever did you want?

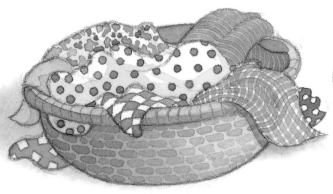

More food? More sleep? Dry clothes? A big cuddle? What a good game that was!

You taught us all to be kind and gentle.

When you fell asleep on someone's lap, they would sit still for ages.

Very quickly, you began to grow up. You learned to sit and smile. No one has a smile quite like yours.

You learned to talk

and to walk.

You learned to climb

and to run.

What an adventurer
you are now!

Every day, you are learning how to do new things all by yourself.

dressing

having friends to play

looking at books

You're even beginning to think of what you might be when you are grown up!

a builder

a painter

a doctor

There are so many things you can dream of being.

an explorer

a park keeper

a dancer

For ever and for always,
you are a very special
person.

For ever and for always,
I will love you: as I have
always loved you since
the day you were born.